THE KINGDOM OF HEAVEN IS LIKE UNTO...

TEN VIRGINS

Narrated by
Maria Lennon

D1523036

The Kingdom of Heaven is like unto…
TEN VIRGINS
Narrated by Maria Lennon
Most scripture verses are KJV or paraphrased

Other books from the Author:
FREE INDEED series:
Book # 1 Set Free
Book # 2 Our Struggle Is Not Against Flesh and Blood

HOSEA, a contemporary historical novella
ELIJAH, Prophet of God, historical fiction

There Is More To Me Than What You See, and Early Childhood
Educational Picture Book

About A Funny Penguin Named Bubbles, by Tirzah Ellis with
Maria Lennon, a story told by a 3-year old

Please address any questions about this book to:
Maria Lennon
Maria.conqueress@gmail.com

**Thy Word is a lamp unto my feet
and a light unto my path.
Psalm 119:105**

There was a town nestled amid mountains all around. The valley was fertile, and people from all over the world came to settle there.

The little town grew larger and larger, with businesses of all sorts; Restaurants, Churches, Shopping Centers, Bars, Movie Theaters, and more. The hustling and bustling of the people awoke early in the mornings and went into the deep of the nights.

In one of the suburbs, ten beautiful young virgins grew up together. And as a matter of fact, they did everything together, such as going to school, sewing their clothes, and playing.

One day, a traveling storyteller came through the valley and told fascinating tales. Many people gathered around him and listened to him. Also, the ten virgins listened curiously.

The traveler told stories about a kingdom without end, with no tears, no violence, no sorrow, and no pain. And he told the people that only the ones with pure hearts could enter this kingdom.

The people who listened were eager to know how to attain a pure heart, knowing that each and everyone sometimes had done wrong. The Creator authored a book of many books written by His believers throughout time. One of the books is Romans, and it says in chapter 3, verse 23: "All have sinned and come short of the glory of the King and His Kingdom."

The people wrung their hands in anguish, some knowing that by their strength, they couldn't just wash their hearts with soap and water to make the uncleanness go away. They cried out, "What must we do to get a clean heart to enter this kingdom without end?"

The storyteller told them about the Creator, who loved everyone, and even though we all have sinned, he sent his son to die on the cross. He did that for all of our sins. And on the third day, he became alive again. When we believe in him, his blood will wash away our sins also. And he is the bridegroom who will call everyone to himself when it is time to enter this kingdom without end.

When some of the people heard this, they were offended by the story and left the storyteller saying pridefully, "I can do good to my fellow neighbor by myself, and my heart will be clean." Others said, "I've never done anything wrong in my whole life. I have a pure heart." And others said, "I have everything I need, this man is telling fairytales, why should I believe him?"

But a good number of people remained and among them were the ten virgins. The storyteller asked them, "Do you believe that the Creator sent his son to die in your stead for the forgiveness of your sins? He is making a way for you to come to him and dwell in the kingdom without end."

The people nodded their heads, each saying, "Yes, I believe." The ten friends hooked arms together, and as one, they said, "Yes, we believe."

The storyteller smiled and, in his gentleness, gave each person a book and said, "The author of this book is the Creator of all things. You are forgiven because you believe, now you have a pure heart. And to keep your heart pure, get to know the Creator's thoughts and words by reading the book and learning what path He has destined for each of you to live."

The people each took the book carefully like a precious treasure. The ten virgins also each got a book. Happiness was beaming from their faces, "Thank you."

The storyteller nods with satisfaction, and then he opens his book and takes out many oil lamps and gives one to everyone.

He tells them, "These are oil lamps showing you the way you must go to keep your heart pure. Even if you mess up, the words from this book will get you back on track. When you read the Creator's book, you will grow in wisdom and understanding, which turns into precious oil and fills the oil lamps. The more you learn of the Creator and his ways, the more oil will flow into your oil lamps and into a special compartment that stores the overflow of oil. Thus, your light will shine brightly and not go out."

The people and the ten virgins thanked the traveling storyteller and went to their houses. The storyteller calls after them, "Remember, be diligent, the bridegroom will be coming for you one day, to lead you into the kingdom without end." Then he goes his way.

And from this day forth, many read in the book of the Creator and learned of him. But the days and months went by, business and obligations took the time of reading, and some people forgot the book after a while.

Five of the ten virgins got bored with the book of the Creator. Two wanted to go out into the town with all the electric lights and do other things. They invited their friends, "Come, let us go out and dance and have a good time."

Another foolish one said, "I am going to a meeting with this new way they are teaching. It sounds interesting."

One wise virgin replies, "The King is our way, the truth, and the life. Don't go there, it's not safe."

Another foolish virgin joins in, "I'll go with you. I need a change anyway."

And the fifth foolish virgin says, "I haven't been on Facebook and Social Media today. I've got to check in with my friends and tell them all about my new clothes. I can do that in town and come along."

The five wise virgins shook their heads. They didn't want to go out dancing, saying, "I would rather read in the book of our Creator. It tells me about how much he loves us. I love his wisdom and how he is protecting us from harm."

The foolish ones said, "There is no harm in having a little fun."

One of the wise ones said, "I have fun reading the book of the Creator." Then she warned, "What about if the bridegroom comes, and you're not ready for him?"

One of the foolish answered, "It was such a long time ago, and he hasn't come yet. Who knows, he might not come at all."

One wise virgin said, "He will come because it says so in this book. We have work to do. Our neighbor is sick, and we must go and cook for him and read to him from the Creator's book."

The second wise virgin said. "We have clothes for the children of the homeless and want to deliver them tonight."

Another of the wise ones said, "And we baked all this bread today for them. We need to bring it over."

Another wise virgin says, "We promised a little girl to visit her father in prison. She wants to know that he is all right. We have an extra book of the Creator and will read some passages to him before we give it to him."

The five wise virgins took their bags with clothing, bread baskets, and their oil lamps, and headed on their way doing the words of the Creator written in the book.

The five foolish virgins laughed at them and ran along to the electric lights of town.

After all their work, the wise virgins arrived home late at night; they fell asleep exhausted.

The foolish ones came home, their hair in disarray, kicking their shoes off and dropping onto their beds, falling asleep.

At midnight there came a shout which everyone heard, "Look, the bridegroom is here! Come out and meet him."

The ten virgins awoke and grabbed their oil lamps. The wise virgins had plenty of extra oil in the overflow. But the foolish virgins realized that their oil lamps weren't bright enough, and they feared that the oil would be running out. They asked the wise virgins, "Give us some of your oil, that our lamps will not go out." But the wise virgins answered. "No, there won't be enough for you and us. Go instead to those who sell oil and buy some for yourselves."

The foolish virgins ran to town.

The wise virgins followed the call and met the bridegroom, who let them into the wedding banquet. There were others with oil lamps who joined them as well. Then the door shut.

After a long while, the foolish virgins arrived at the closed door and knocked. "Lord, Lord! Let us in!" But the bridegroom replied, "I tell you the truth, I don't know you."

And the foolish virgins cried, "We should have read the book of the Creator more, to get to know him better. We didn't listen to the good warnings of our friends to stay alert and be ready for him. We shouldn't have been so selfish. And Facebook and the Internet isn't going to help us either."

Another of the foolish virgins said, "I shouldn't have listened to the new teachers who turned the words of the creator into a self-promoting doctrine. They lied, and I believed it."

Oh, these five foolish virgins were so sad and regretted their ignorance.

The moral of the story is Isaiah 55:6
Seek the Lord while He may be found.
Call upon him while He is near.

And: James 4:8 Draw near to God and
He will draw near to you.

Here is a simple prayer:
Oh Lord God, I make you King of my
heart. I believe that you took my sins
and died for me on the cross. And on
the third day, you rose from the dead.
You died for me that I might live.
Please help me always to ask you first
before I make any decisions. And
please help me daily to read and
understand your Word and learn of
you.

Hebrews 4:12 "Your Word is alive and powerful and sharper than any two-edged sword piercing even to the dividing asunder of the soul and spirit and the joints and marrow and is a discerner of the thoughts and intents of the heart."

When we read the Holy Bible, scripture often jumps off the page, and we are revived or sometimes realize that we must work out something within ourselves. In other words, when we read the Holy Bible, the Word of God reads us and opens our spiritual understanding if we accept it.

*God loves us like a father. We may think that we know God, but He is bigger than anything that will come to our minds. There are many temptations and snares in this world which will hurt us one way or another, but if we honor God as most important in our lives, He will lead us into the way of our destiny and fulfillment.

The last words Jesus told his disciples and, therefore, us, Mark 16:15-17, "Go ye into all the world and preach the gospel to every creature. He that believeth and is baptized shall be saved, and he that believeth not shall be damned. And these signs shall follow them that believe in my name shall they cast out devils; they shall speak with new tongues…"

This little story was inspired by the scripture when Jesus was speaking about the end times:

Matthew 25:1-13

1 "At that time, the kingdom of heaven will be like ten virgins who took their lamps and went out to meet the bridegroom.

2 Five of the virgins were foolish, and five were wise.

3 When the foolish ones took their lamps, they did not take extra olive oil with them.

4 But the wise ones took flasks of olive oil with their lamps.

5 When the bridegroom delayed for a long time, they all became drowsy and fell asleep.

6 But at midnight there was a shout, 'Look, the bridegroom is here! Come out to meet him.'

7 Then all the virgins woke up and trimmed their lamps.

8 The foolish ones said to the wise, 'Give us some of your oil because our lamps are going out.'

9 'No,' they replied. 'There won't be enough for you and us. Go instead to those who sell oil and buy some for yourselves.'

10 But while they had gone to buy it, the bridegroom arrived, and those who were ready went inside with him to the

wedding banquet. Then the door was shut.

11 Later, the other virgins came too, saying, 'Lord, Lord! Let us in!'

12 But he replied, 'I tell you the truth, I do not know you!'

13 Therefore stay alert because you do not know the day or the hour.

Made in the USA
San Bernardino, CA
22 January 2020